2

The Great Stone Face

人面巨石

Original Author   Nathaniel Hawthorne
Adaptors   Louise Benette / David Hwang
Illustrator   Petra Hanzak

WORDS
450

MP3

Let's Enjoy Masterpieces!

All the beautiful fairy tales and masterpieces that you have encountered during your childhood remain as warm memories in your adulthood. This time, let's indulge in the world of masterpieces through English. You can enjoy the depth and beauty of original works, which you can't enjoy through Chinese translations.

The stories are easy for you to understand because of your familiarity with them. When you enjoy reading, your ability to understand English will also rapidly improve.

This series of *Let's Enjoy Masterpieces* is a special reading comprehension booster program, devised to improve reading comprehension for beginners whose command of English is not satisfactory, or who are elementary, middle, and high school students. With this program, you can enjoy reading masterpieces in English with fun and efficiency.

This carefully planned program is composed of 5 levels, from the beginner level of 350 words to the intermediate and advanced levels of 1,000 words. With this program's level-by-level system, you are able to read famous texts in English and to savor the true pleasure of the world's language.

The program is well conceived, composed of reader-friendly explanations of English expressions and grammar, quizzes to help the student learn vocabulary and understand the meaning of the texts, and fabulous illustrations that adorn every page. In addition, with our "Guide to Listening," not only is reading comprehension enhanced but also listening comprehension skills are highlighted.

In the audio recording of the book, texts are vividly read by professional American actors. The texts are rewritten, according to the levels of the readers by an expert editorial staff of native speakers, on the basis of standard American English with the ministry of education recommended vocabulary. Therefore, it will be of great help even for all the students that want to learn English.

Please indulge yourself in the fun of reading and listening to English through *Let's Enjoy Masterpieces*.

霍桑　Nathaniel Hawthorne
(1804-1864)

Nathaniel Hawthorne was an American writer and grew up in a very strict Puritan family. In his childhood, Hawthorne began to take a great interest in reading. After his graduation from college, Hawthorne started his writing career and contributed articles and short stories to the periodicals in his hometown.

In 1837, his first novel was published, which established Hawthorne as a leading writer. He went on to write *The Scarlet Letter* in 1850. Hawthorne is known as a writer who endeavored to probe the interaction between guilt and the human conscience. He provided insight into sins against humanity and internal conflicts.

Hawthorne followed the tradition of his Puritan ancestors and closely dealt with humanity's sinful nature. He used the moral, religious, and psychological perspectives to view the psyche and behavior of individuals who are influenced by selfish solitude and decay.

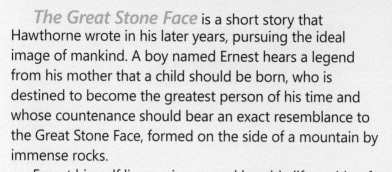

The Great Stone Face is a short story that Hawthorne wrote in his later years, pursuing the ideal image of mankind. A boy named Ernest hears a legend from his mother that a child should be born, who is destined to become the greatest person of his time and whose countenance should bear an exact resemblance to the Great Stone Face, formed on the side of a mountain by immense rocks.

Ernest himself lives a sincere and humble life, waiting for the mountain image to be fulfilled in a living person. As time goes on, he meets a rich merchant, a heroic military man, and a poet. But none of them come close to that of the mountain image.

One day, a poet who is watching Ernest speak to the people of the village proclaims, "Look at Ernest. He resembles the Great Stone Face!" However, on the way back home, Ernest prays that some wiser and better man than himself would appear, bearing a resemblance to the Great Stone Face.

Hawthorne wrote many works that contain moral themes. *The Great Stone Face* is one of those works. The value of a great person does not depend on worldly fame, riches, and power, but on constant self-observation, because an individual's speech and thoughts should also match his or her actions in daily life.

HOW TO USE THIS BOOK
本書使用說明

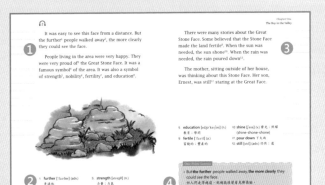

① Original English texts

It is easy to understand the meaning of the text, because the text is rewritten according to the levels of the readers.

② Explanation of the vocabulary

The words and expressions that include vocabulary above the elementary level are clearly defined.

③ Response notes

Spaces are included in the book so you can take notes about what you don't understand or what you want to remember.

④ One point lesson

In-depth analyses of major grammar points and expressions help you to understand sentences with difficult grammar.

∩ *Audio Recording*

In the audio recording, native speakers narrate the texts in standard American English. By combining the written words and the audio recording, you can listen to English with great ease.

Audio books have been popular in Britain and America for many decades. They allow the listener to experience the proper word pronunciation and sentence intonation that add important meaning and drama to spoken English. Students will benefit from listening to the recording twenty or more times.

After you are familiar with the text and recording, listen once more with your eyes closed to check your listening comprehension. Finally, after you can listen with your eyes closed and understand every word and every sentence, you are then ready to mimic the native speaker.

Then you should make a recording by reading the text yourself. Then play both recordings to compare your oral skills with those of a native speaker.

HOW TO IMPROVE
READING ABILITY
如何增進英文閱讀能力

1 Catch key words

Read the key words in the sentences and practice catching the gist of the meaning of the sentence. You might question how working with a few important words could enhance your reading ability. However, it's quite effective. If you continue to use this method, you will find out that the key words and your knowledge of people and situations enables you to understand the sentence.

2 Divide long sentences

Read in chunks of meaning, dividing sentences into meaningful chunks of information. In the book, chunks are arranged in sentences according to meaning. If you consider the sentences backwards or grammatically, your reading speed will be slow and you will find it difficult to listen to English.

You are ready to move to a more sophisticated level of comprehension when you find that narrowly focusing on chunks is irritating. Instead of considering the chunks, you will make it a habit to read the sentence from the beginning to the end to figure out the meaning of the whole.

③ Make inferences and assumptions

Making inferences and assumptions is part of your ability. If you don't know, try to guess the meaning of the words. Although you don't know all the words in context, don't go straight to the dictionary. Developing an ability to make inferences in the context is important.

The first way to figure out the meaning of a word is from its context. If you cannot make head or tail out of the meaning of a word, look at what comes before or after it. Ask yourself what can happen in such a situation. Make your best guess as to the word's meaning. Then check the explanations of the word in the book or look up the word in a dictionary.

④ Read a lot and reread the same book many times

There is no shortcut to mastering English. Only if you do a lot of reading will you make your way to the summit. Read fun and easy books with an average of less than one new word per page. Try to immerse yourself in English as often as you can.

Spend time "swimming" in English. Language learning research has shown that immersing yourself in English will help you improve your English, even though you may not be aware of what you're learning.

CONTENTS

Before You Read

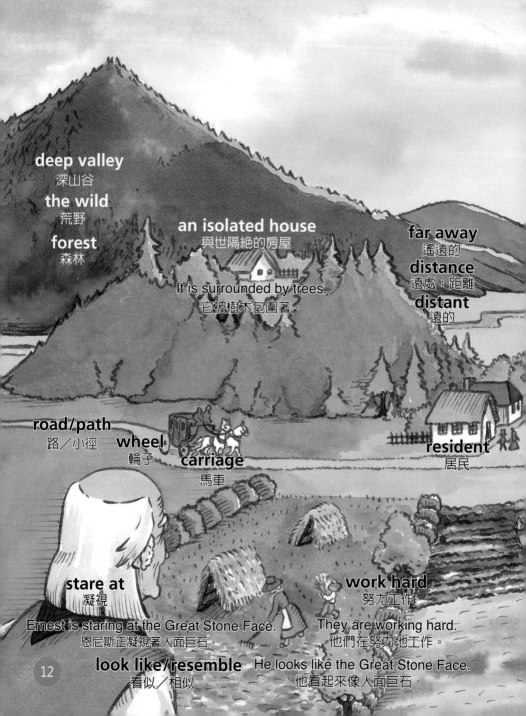

deep valley
深山谷

the wild
荒野

forest
森林

an isolated house
與世隔絕的房屋

It is surrounded by trees.
它被樹木包圍著。

far away
遙遠的

distance
遠處；距離

distant
遠的

road/path
路／小徑

wheel
輪子

carriage
馬車

resident
居民

stare at
凝視

Ernest is staring at the Great Stone Face.
恩尼斯正凝視著人面巨石。

look like/resemble
看似／相似

work hard
努力工作

They are working hard.
他們在努力地工作。

He looks like the Great Stone Face.
他看起來像人面巨石。

The Great Stone Face
人面巨石

giant / huge / grand
巨大的

legendary
傳說的

symbol of the area
地區的象徵

nobility 高貴；貴族

fertility 肥沃

wisdom 才智

intelligence 智慧

education 教育

a mass of rocks
一堆岩石

sunset
日落；黃昏

rays of sun
陽光

The sun is setting.
太陽升起。

wooden house 木屋

log cabin 木屋

a local village
當地村落

hut
小屋

barn
穀倉

A farmer is leading a horse.
農夫正領著一匹馬往前行。

crops
作物

grain
穀物

A man is plowing a field.
一名男子正在犁田。

barley
大麥

wheat
小麥

corn
玉米

fertile
豐饒的

rice
米

rich field
肥沃的　田地

13

Chapter One

🎧 The Boy in the Valley

Deep in a valley[1], there was a pretty little house. It was surrounded by[2] many tall trees. Sitting in front of their small home, a mother and her young son were watching the sun go down[3].

"It is a very beautiful evening, isn't it?" the mother asked the boy. He just nodded[4]. He was staring at[5] something in the distance[6].

1. **valley** [ˈvæli] (n.) 山谷；溪谷
2. **be surrounded by** 被⋯⋯環繞
3. **go down** 落下
4. **nod** [nɑːd] (v.) 點頭
5. **stare at** 凝視
6. **in the distance** 在遠處
7. **far away** 遙遠

Very far away[7], they could see the Great Stone Face. They were many miles from it, but they could see it clearly[8].

It was an amazing[9] sight[10]. It looked like[11] a sculpture[12] of a giant[13] in the rocks. The Face had a long nose and big lips and eyes. It was a very noble[14] face.

8. **clearly** [`klɪrli] (adv.) 清楚地
9. **amazing** [ə`meɪzɪŋ] (a.) 驚人的
10. **sight** [saɪt] (n.) 景色；景象
11. **look like** 看似
12. **sculpture** [`skʌlptʃər] (n.) 雕像；雕刻品
13. **giant** [`dʒaɪənt] (n.) 巨人
14. **noble** [`noubəl] (a.) 高貴的；崇高的

It was easy to see this face from a distance. But the further[1] people walked away[2], the more clearly they could see the face.

People living in the area were very happy. They were very proud of[3] the Great Stone Face. It was a famous symbol[4] of the area. It was also a symbol of strength[5], nobility[6], fertility[7], and education[8].

1. **further** [ˋfɝːrðər] (adv.)
   更遠地
2. **walk away** 走離開
3. **be proud of** 以……為傲
4. **symbol** [ˋsɪmbəl] (n.)
   象徵；標誌

5. **strength** [strɛŋθ] (n.)
   力量；力氣
6. **nobility** [noʊˋbɪləti] (n.)
   高貴；高尚
7. **fertility** [fərˋtɪləti] (n.)
   （土地的）肥沃

There were many stories about the Great Stone Face. Some believed that the Stone Face made the land fertile[9]. When the sun was needed, the sun shone[10]. When the rain was needed, the rain poured down[11].

The mother, sitting outside of her house, was thinking about this Stone Face. Her son, Ernest, was still[12] staring at the Great Face.

8. **education** [edʒəˋkeɪʃən] (n.) 教育；學問
9. **fertile** [ˋfɜːrtl] (a.) 富饒的；豐產的
10. **shine** [ʃaɪn] (v.) 發光；照耀 (shine-shone-shone)
11. **pour down** 下大雨
12. **still** [stɪl] (adv.) 仍然；還

One Point Lesson

● But **the further** people walked away, **the more clearly** they could see the face.
但人們走得越遠，就越能清楚看見那張臉。

「**the + 比較級 , the + 比較級**」：表示「越⋯⋯，就越⋯⋯」。

e.g. **The more** you practice, **the higher** you can jump.
你練習越多次，就可以跳得越高。

🎧 3

He turned to[1] her now and said, "Mother,
Great Stone Face looks[2] so kind and smart[3].
If it could speak, it would have a very kind voice.
I want to meet a man like him."

His mother said, "A very old story says that
one day[4] a man like him will be born[5]. Did you
hear this story?"

The boy excitedly[6] said, "No, mother!
I haven't! Please tell me."

The mother began to tell her son the story.

"It began a long time ago[7]. Long ago, many Indian[8] people lived in this valley. They believed that one day a child would be born. The child would have a great destiny[9]. He would be one of the smartest, richest and noblest men. He would also look like the Great Stone Face.

Many people are waiting for the child to be born. Others think it is only a story. Whatever[10] people believe, it has not happened yet."

1. **turn to** 向……轉身
2. **look** [lʊk] (v.) 看起來
3. **smart** [smɑːrt] (a.) 聰明的
4. **one day** 某一天
5. **be born** 出生
6. **excitedly** [ɪkˋsaɪtɪdli] (adv.) 興奮地

7. **a long time ago** 很久以前
8. **Indian** [ˋɪndɪən] (a.) 印地安人的
9. **destiny** [ˋdestɪni] (n.) 命運
10. **whatever** [wɑːtˋevər] (pron.) 不管什麼

One Point Lesson

◆ He would be **one of the smartest, richest, and noblest men.**
他會是最聰明、最富有、最高貴的一個人。

---

one of the . . . : 其中一個……。後接複數名詞。

🔊 She is **one of the prettiest girls** in our school.
她是我們學校最漂亮的女生之一。

The boy listened very carefully¹ to his mother. "Mother! I really hope² it will happen. I want to see the man. I know I will really like him."

The mother didn't believe the story, but she wanted to give hope to her son. So she said, "It might³ happen. One day soon, it might happen."

The little boy never forgot⁴ that story. Every day, he woke up⁵ and looked at the Stone Face. He hoped he would meet the man who looked like the Great Stone Face.

1. **carefully** [ˋkerfəli] (adv.)
   小心地；謹慎地
2. **hope** [houp] (v.) 希望
3. **might** [maɪt] (aux.)
   用來表示「可能」的助動詞
4. **forget** [fərˋget] (v.) 忘記
   (forget-forgot-forgotten)
5. **wake up** 醒來；起床
6. **obey** [əˋbeɪ] (v.) 服從；聽話

Ernest was a wonderful little boy. He loved his mother very much. He always helped her. He always obeyed[6] his mother. But the biggest help was his love for her.

Ernest quickly grew up[1].
He spent many days
working in the fields[2]. He
was always loving[3] and
devoted[4].
He was also very smart.

He did not have a
good education[5], but
some people said,
"Ernest is so smart.
Many boys study at
famous schools. But Ernest is smarter than all of
them. He has such wisdom[6]. He will be a great
man one day."

1. **grow up** 成長
   (grow-grew-grown)
2. **field** [fi:ld] (n.) 田地
3. **loving** [`lʌvɪŋ] (a.) 親愛的
4. **devoted** [dɪ`voutɪd] (a.)
   奉獻的
5. **have a good education**
   受良好教育
6. **wisdom** [`wɪzdəm] (n.) 智慧

7. **all day** 整天
8. **develop** [dɪ`veləp] (v.)
   逐漸養成；發展
9. **clear** [klɪr] (a.) 清楚的
10. **hate** [heɪt] (n.) 仇恨
11. **jealousy** [`dʒeləsi] (n.) 嫉妒
12. **calm** [kɑ:m] (a.) 平靜的
13. **attitude** [`ætɪtu:d] (n.) 態度

Usually, after working very hard all day[7], Ernest went to look at the Great Stone Face. He sat quietly for hours just watching it.

During this time, he thought about many things. He developed[8] clear[9] ideas about life.

He sat thinking about hate[10], pain, jealousy[11] and many other things in life. But the most important thing he thought about was love. He developed a calm[12] and loving attitude[13] for all things.

One Point Lesson

◊ He spent many days working in the fields.
他花了很多時間在田裡工作。

「spend + 時間 + V-ing」：花……時間做……

e.g. He spent three hours playing basketball with his friends.
他花了三小時與朋友打籃球。

A Circle the words related to the Great Stone Face.

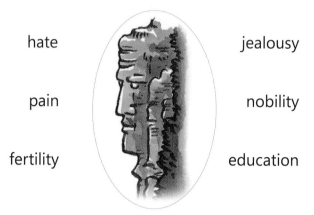

hate

pain

fertility

jealousy

nobility

education

B True or False.

T F **1** All of the people living in the valley were farmers.

T F **2** The Great Stone Face was a symbol of the valley.

T F **3** Ernest lived with his mother and two brothers.

T F **4** Ernest thought many things about life.

C Choose the correct answer.

1 What was the legend of the Great Stone Face?

(a) Every crop in the valley will be great.

(b) A man resembling the Great Stone Face will be born.

(c) Every person living in the valley will become famous one day.

2 What did Ernest thought the most?

(a) Mathematics and history

(b) Love for other people

(c) How to make a lot of money

D Fill in the blanks.

stare at	wait for

1 Ernest was _____ something in the distance.

2 Many people _____ the child to be born.

Chapter Two

🎧 A Rich Businessman

One day, Ernest was working in his fields. Suddenly[1], a neighbor[2] came to him and asked, "Did you hear the news?"

"No. What news?" Ernest replied.

The neighbor continued[3], "People say that there is a great man in Newport. He looks like the Great Stone Face. People call[4] him Mr. Gathergold. But I don't think that's his real name. Anyway, a long time ago, he used to[5] live in this valley. He moved to[6] Newport and started a business."

Ernest was very happy to hear this news. Ernest asked, "Why do people call him Mr. Gathergold?"

The neighbor said, "Well, long ago, he was very poor. But he started a business with just a little money. He is very smart and became very wealthy[7].

He trades with[8] people in many countries. From Africa, he brings back[9] gold and diamonds. From Asia, he buys carpets. He also brings back spices[10], many kinds of[11] tea, and also pearls[12]."

1. **suddenly** [`sʌdnli] (adv.) 忽然地
2. **neighbor** [`neɪbər] (n.) 鄰居
3. **continue** [kən`tɪnjuː] (v.) 繼續
4. **call** *A B*：把 A 稱為 B
5. **used to** 曾經
6. **move to** 搬到
7. **wealthy** [`welθi] (a.) 富裕的
8. **trade with** 與……交易
9. **bring back** 帶回
10. **spice** [spaɪs] (n.) 香料
11. **many kind of** 各種類的……
12. **pearl** [pɜːrl] (n.) 珍珠

One Point Lesson

◆ Anyway, a long time ago, he **used to live** in this valley.
反正很久以前,他曾經住在這個山谷中。

used to + 動詞原形：表示過去的習慣或行為。

e.g. Mike **used to be** a good student. 麥克過去是個好學生。

"He is a very successful[1] man," continued the neighbor.

"Some compare him to[2] Midas. You know the Greek[3] story of Midas, don't you? Everything Midas touched[4] turned to[5] gold. Well, some people say that everything Mr. Gathergold touches becomes gold. Anyway, there is a rumor[6] now in the valley. Maybe[7] Mr. Gathergold will return[8] here."

Ernest was very interested[9] to hear this.

"He has so much money now. I heard he might return to his native[10] valley, and build a large house. You know that really beautiful area beside the river next to the Johnson's house? A long time ago, Mr. Gathergold grew up there. People said there were plans to build a huge[11] house there."

"Really!" Ernest said. "I want to see this man. I hope he really looks like the Great Stone Face."

1. **successful** [sək`sesfəl] (a.)
   成功的
2. **compare** A **to** B 把 A 比作 B
3. **Greek** [gri:k] (a.) 希臘的
4. **touch** [tʌtʃ] (v.) 觸摸
5. **turn to** 變為
6. **rumor** [`ru:mər] (n.)
   謠言；傳聞
7. **maybe** [`meɪbi] (aux.)
   可能；或許
8. **return** [rɪ`tɜ:rn] (v.) 返回
9. **interested** [`ɪntrəstɪd] (a.)
   感興趣的
10. **native** [`neɪtɪv] (a.) 家鄉的
11. **huge** [hju:dʒ] (a.) 巨大的

Many weeks passed, and many builders[1] came to the valley. They started to build a house beside the river. Many people came to watch them make the amazing[2] house.

After many months, the house was finished. It was the most talked-about[3] thing in the valley.

"Did you see the house?" people asked Ernest.

"Yes, I did," Ernest replied. "Isn't it amazing? Mr. Gathergold must be the man we have waited for."

The building was really amazing. From a distance[4], it seemed to be a white shining star. When a person walked closer, one could see huge pillars[5] at the front. It was made from[6] very expensive marble[7].

At the front, there was a huge door. It was made from the finest[8] imported[9] wood, and had the most beautiful door knobs[10].

1. **builder** [ˋbɪldər] (n.)
   建築商；建築工人
2. **amazing** [əˋmeɪzɪŋ] (a.)
   令人吃驚的
3. **be talked-about** 被談論的
4. **from a distance** 從遠處
5. **pillar** [ˋpɪlər] (n.) 柱子
6. **be made from** 由……製造
7. **marble** [ˋmɑːrbəl] (n.) 大理石
8. **fine** [faɪn] (a.) 上等的
9. **imported** [ˋɪmpɔːrtɪd] (a.)
   進口的
10. **knob** [nɑːb] (n.)（圓形）把手

One Point Lesson

◆ Many people came to **watch them make** the amazing house. 很多人前來看他們建造這棟驚人的房屋。

watch A + 動詞原形：看 A 做某事。

→ see、hear、watch 屬於感官動詞，A 後面的動詞為其補語，必須用主動。

e.g. The teacher **saw the boy listen** to the music in class.
老師看見男孩在課堂上聽音樂。

Everyone was very curious[1] about this house. "What does it look like inside?" they wondered[2].

One man, a builder, said, "It is more beautiful inside than outside. The furniture, carpets, and curtains are all imported. Mr. Gathergold's bedroom is the most amazing. There is gold everywhere. It sparkles[3] so much. I guess[4] he couldn't sleep without gold around him."

1. **curious** [ˈkjʊriəs] (a.) 好奇的
2. **wonder** [ˈwʌndə(r)] (v.) 想知道
3. **sparkle** [ˈspɑːrkəl] (v.) 閃耀
4. **guess** [ɡes] (v.) 猜測
5. **include** [ɪnˈkluːd] (v.) 包括；包含
6. **be ready to** 準備好做……
7. **accept** A **as** B 接受 A 成為 B

Everyone, including[5] Ernest, was ready to[6] accept Mr. Gathergold as[7] the legendary[8] man. They all waited for his arrival[9].

In the valley, many people asked, "When will he arrive?"

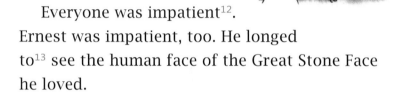

"He is expected to[10] arrive at sunset[11] today," others replied.

Everyone was impatient[12]. Ernest was impatient, too. He longed to[13] see the human face of the Great Stone Face he loved.

Ernest thought, "When he comes, he will do great things for the valley. He is rich, so he can do great things."

---

8. **legendary** [ˋlɛdʒənˌdɛri] (a.) 傳說的

9. **arrival** [əˋraɪvəl] (n.) 抵達

10. **be expected to** 被預期會⋯⋯

11. **at sunset** 日落時

12. **impatient** [ɪmˋpeɪʃənt] (a.) 不耐煩的

13. **long to** 渴望

Sunset came, and many people gathered[1] to wait for the famous man. Ernest was waiting with them. Suddenly, there was the noise[2] of wheels[3] moving along[4] the road.

"He is coming! He is coming!" someone cried. "He has finally[5] arrived!"

As[6] the carriage[7] passed by[8], Ernest saw the man. He was very old, and had small eyes and thin lips.

"He looks just like the Great Stone Face," some shouted. "Now great things will come to us here in this valley!"

1. **gather** [ˋgæðəːr] (v.) 聚集
2. **noise** [nɔɪz] (n.) 喧鬧聲
3. **wheel** [wiːl] (n.) 車輪
4. **along** [əˋlɔːŋ] (prep.) 沿著
5. **finally** [ˋfaɪnəli] (adv.) 最後
6. **as** [əz] (conj.) 當……時
7. **carriage** [ˋkærɪdʒ] (n.) 馬車
8. **pass by** 經過
9. **ahead** [əˋhed] (adv.) 在前
10. **beg** [beg] (v.) 乞討
11. **on the side of** 在……邊
12. **poke** [pouk] (v.) 伸出

Ernest watched the carriage go down the road. Ahead[9], there was an old woman and two little children. They were begging[10] on the side of[11] the road.

As the carriage passed them, Ernest saw a yellow hand poke[12] through the window. The hand threw out[13] a few copper[14] coins at the beggars[15].

Ernest was now very disappointed[16].

13. **throw out** 拋出；丟出
14. **copper** [`kɑːpər] (a.) 銅（製）的
15. **beggar** [`begər] (n.) 乞丐
16. **disappointed** [dɪsə`pɔɪntɪd] (a.) 失望的

But still people cried out[1], "He looks just like the Great Stone Face!"

Ernest thought, "He may look like the Great Stone Face on the outside[2], but his heart does not resemble[3] him at all[4]. The old man seemed cold, and selfish[5]. But the Great Stone Face is generous[6] and kind."

Then, he turned to look at the Great Stone Face. The Stone Face seemed to speak to him at that moment. He said, "Do not worry, Ernest. One day, he will come."

1. **cry out** 喊叫；大聲說
2. **outside** [aut`saɪd] (n.) 外表
3. **resemble** [rɪ`zembəl] (v.) 像；類似
4. **not . . . at all** 完全不⋯⋯
5. **selfish** [`selfɪʃ] (a.) 自私的
6. **generous** [`dʒenərəs] (a.) 慷慨的
7. **in fact** 事實上
8. **silly** [`sɪli] (a.) 愚蠢的
9. **neglect** [nɪ`glekt] (v.) 忽略
10. **daily** [`deɪli] (a.) 每日的

Many years passed by, and Ernest grew into a man. But every day, he still spent time looking at the Stone Face.

In fact[7] some people said, "Ernest still spends so much time looking at the Great Stone Face. It is a little silly[8]."

Other people said, "Let him do it. He does not neglect[9] his daily[10] work."

One Point Lesson

◆ He **may** look like the Great Stone Face on the outside.
他或許外表看起來像人面巨石。

---

may 與動詞原形連用,表示「**可能性**」,且 may 的拼法不會隨人稱變化。

e.g. She is absent. She **may** be sick.
她今天缺席,可能是生病了。

37

But nobody really knew Ernest. The Great Stone Face taught[1] him many things. The things he knew, he could never learn[2] from a book.

From the inspiration[3] of the Stone Face, he developed his knowledge[4], his way of life[5], and his character[6].

He was one of the wisest men on earth[7]. But even[8] Ernest didn't know that yet.

Many more years passed by. Mr. Gathergold died one day. All of his money disappeared[9] just before he died.

Everyone thought, "What happened to his money?" But these questions were never answered. After a while[10], people did not compare him to the Great Face.

Eventually[11], he only became famous for[12] one thing—his very large home. This became a hotel. In the summer many people stayed[13] there, and went to see the Great Stone Face.

1. **teach** [ti:tʃ] (v.) 教導
   (teach-taught-taught)
2. **learn** [lɜ:rn] (v.) 學習
3. **inspiration** [ɪnspə`reɪʃən] (n.)
   靈感
4. **knowledge** [`nɑ:lɪdʒ] (n.)
   知識
5. **way of life** 生活方式
6. **character** [`kærəktər] (n.)
   性格；特質
7. **on earth** 世界上
8. **even** [`i:vən] (adv.) 甚至；連
9. **disappear** [dɪsə`pɪr] (v.) 消失
10. **after a while** 過了一陣子
11. **eventually** [ɪ`ventʃuəli] (adv.)
    最後地；終於地
12. **famous for** 因……出名
13. **stay** [steɪ] (v.) 停留
    (stay-stayed-stayed)

Comprehension Quiz Chapter Two

A Answer the following questions.

1 What did Mr. Gathergold start in Newport?

⇨ _____

2 Where did Mr. Gathergold get gold and diamonds?

⇨ _____

3 Whom did people compare Mr. Gathergold to?

⇨ _____

B Fill in the blanks with the antonym of the words underlined.

1 He was smart and became very w_____.

⇔ poor

2 The architects built a h_____ house.

⇔ small

3 The pillars were made from e_____ marble.

⇔ cheap

C True of False.

T F ① Ernest heard about Mr. Gathergold from his neighbor.

T F ② Mr. Gathergold grew up in the valley a long time ago.

T F ③ Everything Mr. Gathergold touched turned to gold.

D Fill in the blanks with the given words.

wood	knobs	star	palace

Mr. Gathergold's new house was really amazing. It was like a ① _____. From a distance, it seemed to be a shining ② _____. The door was made from imported ③ _____ and had very beautiful ④ _____.

gathering 聚會
party 宴會
feast 盛宴
banquet 宴會
celebration 慶祝
parade 遊行

banner
旗幟

WELCOME

placard
公告

door knob
門把

a crowd of people
一群人
citizen
市民

remarkable
President
出色的總統

People are listening to the general.
人們正在聽將軍說話。

curious professor
愛探究的教授

Hurrah !
歡呼聲

rich businessman
富裕的商人

A big table is filled with food and drinks.
大桌上擺滿了食物和飲料。

musical band
樂團

It is playing patriotic songs.
他們正在演奏愛國歌曲。

42

· Chapter Three ·

🎧13 A Great Soldier

Many years ago, another man grew up in the valley. This man left home and joined[1] the army[2]. He became a great soldier[3].

After many years of life in the army, he became a general[4]. He was called[5] Old Blood[6]-and-Thunder[7]. He was now very old. He had many scars[8] from war.

1. **join** [dʒɔɪn] (v.) 參加
2. **army** [ˋɑːrmi] (n.) 軍隊
3. **soldier** [ˋsouldʒər] (n.) 軍人
4. **general** [ˋdʒenərəl] (n.) 將軍
5. **be called** 被稱為
6. **blood** [blʌd] (n.) 血
7. **thunder** [ˋθʌndər] (n.) 雷
8. **scar** [skɑːr] (n.) 疤；傷痕

He was tired of[9] military[10] life, and decided to[11] return to his home in the valley.

One day, Ernest and his neighbor were talking. "Did you hear the latest[12] rumor[13], Ernest?" asked the neighbor.

"Yes. People say the old general resembles the Stone Face," said Ernest. "Is it true?"

"Well, I don't know. But an assistant[14] to the general came here, and said the general looks just like the Great Stone Face," replied the neighbor.

"We will have to[15] wait until[16] he arrives," said Ernest.

9. **be tired of** 對……厭倦
10. **military** [ˋmɪləteri] (a.) 軍隊的
11. **decide to** 決定
12. **latest** [ˋleɪtɪst] (a.) 最近的
13. **rumor** [ˋruːmər] (n.) 傳聞
14. **assistant** [əˋsɪstənt] (n.) 助手
15. **have to** 必須
16. **until** [ənˋtɪl] (conj.) 直到……時

The local[1] townspeople[2] decided to have a large festival[3] to welcome Old Blood-and-Thunder home. When this day came, everyone went to town to join the festival. Ernest went to see the banquet[4].

It was a really beautiful banquet. On the table, a feast[5] was prepared[6]. It looked so delicious. In the distance, people could see the image[7] of the Great Stone Face.

Ernest could see many people gathering around the banquet. He could hear the Reverend[8] Battleblast speaking. Ernest stood on his tiptoes[9] to see Old Blood-and-Thunder. But there were too many people.

He gave up[10] trying to see. Instead[11], he turned to look at the Great Stone Face. He felt comforted[12] by the smile of the Great Stone Face.

1. **local** [ˋloukəl] (a.) 當地的
2. **townspeople** [ˋtaʊnzpiːpəl] (n.) 市民
3. **festival** [ˋfɛstɪvəl] (n.) 節慶
4. **banquet** [ˋbæŋkwɪt] (n.) 盛宴
5. **feast** [fiːst] (n.) 筵席
6. **prepare** [prɪˋper] (v.) 準備
7. **image** [ˋɪmɪdʒ] (n.) 影像
8. **reverend** [ˋrɛvərənd] (n.) 教士；牧師（大寫）
9. **stand on tiptoe** 踮起腳尖
10. **give up** 放棄
11. **instead** [ɪnˋstɛd] (adv.) 取而代之地
12. **comforted** [ˋkʌmfərtɪd] (a.) 安慰的

One Point Lesson

◆ Ernest could see many people gathering around the banquet.
恩尼斯可以見到許多人聚集在宴會上。

「see + A + V-ing」：看見 A 正在做某事，表動作正在進行。

e.g. I saw him reading a comic book. 我看到他在看漫畫。

Ernest stood at the back of[1] the crowd for a while[2]. As he looked at the Great Stone Face, he heard many people around him.

One person said, "He looks exactly[3] like the Great Stone Face!"

Ernest also heard another say, "Old Blood-and-Thunder is the greatest man. He is the Great Stone Face."

These people gave a great shout, "Hurrah[4]!" This encouraged[5] other people to do the same.

After listening to everyone, Ernest thought, "This must be the human form[6] of the Great Stone Face. It must be true!"

1. **at the back of** 在……後面
2. **for a while** 一會兒
3. **exactly** [ɪgˋzæktli] (adv.) 確切地；完全地
4. **hurrah** [həˋrɑː] (n.) 萬歲的歡呼聲
5. **encourage** A **to** 鼓勵 A 做……
6. **form** [fɔːrm] (n.) 外形
7. **a man of war** 好戰的人

However , Ernest had not expected the Great Stone Face would be a man of war[7]. He had expected a man of peace. He had expected a man of wisdom and knowledge. But he thought, "A man of war can still do great things."

One Point Lesson

◆ **A man of war** can still do great things.
好戰的人還是可以做出偉大的事。

「**a man of + 名詞**」：……的人

e.g. a man of **wisdom** 智者   a man of **wealth** 富人
a man of **knowledge** 學識豐富的人 a man of **his word** 誠信的人
a man of **ability** 有能力的人   a man of **blood** 殘暴之人
a man of **few words** 話不多的人   a man of **nobility** 高貴的人

Soon after[1], he heard someone cry out, "The general! It's the general! He is going to[2] make a speech[3]. Everyone! Please be quiet[4]." The crowd became quiet.

Finally, the general stood, and everyone could see him. Old Blood-and-Thunder began to speak. But Ernest was not listening to him. He was looking at the general's face and then his military uniform[5]. It was very splendid[6]. It was dark green and had many badges[7] on it.

Ernest watched him for a while, and then thought, "Does he really resemble[8] the Great Stone Face?"

1. **soon after** 很快地
2. **be going to** 將要
3. **make a speech** 發表演說
4. **quiet** [ˋkwaɪət] (a.) 安靜的
5. **uniform** [ˋjuːnɪfɔːrm] (n.) 制服
6. **splendid** [ˋsplendɪd] (a.) 光彩的；燦爛的
7. **badge** [bædʒ] (n.) 徽章
8. **resemble** [rɪˋzembəl] (v.) 像；相似

Behind[1] the general, Ernest could see the image of the Great Stone Face.

He looked at the Face he loved and thought, "This face has so much wisdom. This face has so much kindness and generosity[2]. Old Blood-and-Thunder's face has none[3] of these. He is not the legendary man. We all must wait longer[4]."
Ernest left the banquet, and went home.

Late that afternoon, he went to sit and watch the Great Face.

The sunshine shone through the clouds casting[5] shadows[6] across[7] the Face. The effect[8] of the shadows created[9] a smile on the Great Face.

1. **behind** [bɪˋhaɪnd] (prep.)
   在……後面
2. **generosity** [dʒɛnəˋrɑːsəti]
   (n.) 寬大；慷慨
3. **none** [nʌn] (pron.) 一個也沒
4. **longer** [ˋlɔːŋɚ] (adv.)
   更久地；是 long 的比較級
5. **cast** [kæst] (v.) 撒
   (cast-cast-cast)
6. **shadow** [ˋʃædoʊ] (n.) 陰影

It gave a lot of comfort[10] to Ernest. In his mind[11], Ernest could hear the Face saying, "Do not worry, Ernest. He will come."

7. **across** [əˋkrɔːs] (prep.) 橫過
8. **effect** [ɪˋfekt] (n.) 效果
9. **create** [kriˋeɪt] (v.) 創造

10. **comfort** [ˋkʌmfərt] (n.) 安慰
11. **mind** [maɪnd] (n.) 內心

Many more years passed by. Ernest grew[1] older and older, and now he was a man of middle age[2]. He was still the same simple-hearted[3] man, and everyone knew and loved him. But he was even[4] wiser now.

1. **grow** [grou] (v.) 漸漸變得
2. **middle age** 中年
3. **simple-hearted**
   [ˋsɪmpəlˌhɑːrtɪd] (a.) 純真的
4. **even** [ˋiːvən] (adv.) 甚至;更

He always tried to do his best[5] for others. Not only did his goodness[6] show in his actions, but also in his speech[7]. He always talked to others very kindly. He gave honest advice[8] to people with problems. He spoke truthfully[9] like no other person could.

Everyone loved Ernest, but no one really knew that Ernest was an extraordinary[10] man.

5. **do one's best** 全力以赴
6. **goodness** [`gʊdnəs] (n.)
   善良；美德
7. **speech** [spiːtʃ] (n.) 演講
8. **advice** [əd`vaɪs] (n.)
   建議；忠告
9. **truthfully** [`truːθfəli] (adv.)
   忠誠地
10. **extraordinary**
    [ɪk`strɔːrdəneri]
    (a.) 不凡的

> One Point Lesson

Not only did his goodness show in his actions, but also in his speech.
他的善良不只表現在行為上，也表現在他的演說中。

「**not only A, but also B**」：不但 A，而且 B

e.g. I like **not only** movies, **but also** plays.
我不只喜歡電影，也喜歡戲劇。

A Circle the odd one among the following groups of words.

1 soldier   angel   army   war

2 feast   banquet   forest   festival

3 kindness   form   sincerity   gentleness

B Choose the correct answer.

1 Old Blood-and-Thunder decided to return to the valley because _____

(a) he had many friends there.

(b) he was tired of military life.

(c) he wanted to make people happy.

2 Ernest gave honest advice _____

(a) to everyone knew and loved him.

(b) to people with problems.

(c) to the world of love.

C Which person are they talking about?
Ernest or Old-Blood-and-Thunder?
Write down "E" for Ernest and "O" for the soldier.

❶ He spoke truthfully like no other person could. (   )

❷ He had many badges to show his success. (   )

❸ He had gentle and pure thoughts. (   )

❹ He returned to live the rest of his life. (   )

D Complete the sentences with the given words.

❶ Ernest did not expect _____

_____.

(man / he / a / war / would be / of)

❷ All of this was just next to a forest _____

_____.

(trees / with / behind / many / the chairs and table)

Chapter Four

🎧 ⟨19⟩ A Famous Politician

Like Mr. Gathergold, Old Blood-and-Thunder passed away[1] as an insignificant[2] man for the valley. Now, many people said, "Old Blood-and-Thunder did not really resemble the Great Stone Face. We were foolish[3] to think so."

But not long after[4], there was a new report[5]. People said another man looked like the Great Face.

This man also grew up in the valley a long time ago. Now, he was a politician[6]. This new man, Old Stony[7] Phiz[8], was not a wealthy man. Also, he was not a soldier. Instead, he was a brilliant[9] speaker.

1. **pass away** 過世
2. **insignificant** [ɪnsɪɡ`nɪfɪkənt] (a.) 無足輕重的
3. **foolish** [`fuːlɪʃ] (a.) 愚蠢的
4. **not long after** 不久之後
5. **report** [rɪ`pɔːrt] (n.) 謠言
6. **politician** [pɑːlə`tɪʃən] (n.) 政治家

He spoke so clearly and well. He could enter any argument[10] and win. In the halls of government[11], people always stopped to listen to him. Old Stony Phiz was respected[12] throughout[13] the country.

7. **stony** [`stouni] (a.)
   堅硬的；冷酷的
8. **phiz** [fɪz] (n.) 臉；相貌
9. **brilliant** [`brɪliənt] (a.) 傑出的
10. **argument** [`ɑːrgjumənt]
    (n.) 辯論

11. **government** [`gʌvərnmənt]
    (n.) 政府
12. **respect** [rɪ`spekt] (v.)
    尊重；敬重
13. **throughout** [θruː`aut] (prep.)
    遍布；處處

One Point Lesson

◆ In the halls of government, people always **stopped to listen** to him.
在政府機構中，人們總會駐足聆聽他說話。

「**stop + to + 動詞原形**」：停下來做……

「**stop + V-ing**」：停止做……

e.g. We **stopped to talk**. 我們停下來講話。

20

Now, Old Stony Phiz wanted to become President[1]. But even before this, people started to say, "Did you look at Old Stony Phiz? He looks just like the Great Stone Face."

So now, people were hopeful[2] that Old Stony Phiz was the legendary man.

One day, when Ernest was working in his fields, his neighbor came to see him.

"Ernest!" he said. "Did you hear the latest reports?"

Ernest replied, "Yes, they say Old Stony Phiz looks like the Great Stone Face."

"He could[3] be the legendary man, you know," said the neighbor.

1. **president** [ˈprɛzɪdənt] (n.) 總統（大寫）
2. **hopeful** [ˈhoupfəl] (a.) 希望的
3. **could** [kʊd] (aux.) 可能
4. **neither** *A* **nor** *B* 不是 A 也不是 B
5. **wait and see** 觀望
6. **go back to** 回到

Ernest thought and said, "Well, neither[4] Mr. Gathergold nor old Blood-and-Thunder was the legendary man. We will have to wait and see[5]."

Then, Ernest went back to[6] working in his fields.

21

During Old Stony Phiz's presidency[1] campaign[2], he went to visit the valley of the Great Stone Face. His only purpose[3] of going there was to gather support[4] for the election[5]. But the residents[6] prepared the greatest celebration[7] for him.

A wonderful parade[8] was organized[9]. That day, everyone left their work and went to see Old Stony Phiz. Ernest did too. Even though[10] there were many disappointments[11], he was always hopeful.

Along the road into the town, crowds of[12] people gathered.

After they had waited for some time, the great man came riding[13] along the road with other great men. There were so many people, and so many men riding on the dusty[14] road. The dust[15] from the road made it impossible[16] to see anything clearly.

1. **presidency** [ˈprɛzɪdənsi] (n.) 總統職位
2. **campaign** [kæmˈpeɪn] (n.) 競選活動
3. **purpose** [ˈpɜːrpəs] (n.) 目的
4. **support** [səˈpɔːrt] (n.) 支持
5. **election** [ɪˈlɛkʃən] (n.) 選舉
6. **resident** [ˈrɛzɪdənt] (n.) 居民
7. **celebration** [sɛlɪˈbreɪʃən] (n.) 慶祝

8. **parade** [pə`reɪd] (n.) 遊行
9. **organize** [`ɔːrgənaɪz] (v.)
   組織;安排
10. **even though** 即使;雖然
11. **disappointment** [dɪsə`pɔɪntmənt]
    (n.) 失望
12. **crowds of** 許多（人）

13. **ride** [raɪd] (v.) 騎馬
14. **dusty** [`dʌsti] (a.)
    滿是灰塵的
15. **dust** [dʌst] (n.) 塵埃
16. **impossible** [ɪm`pɑːsəbəl] (a.)
    不可能的

One Point Lesson

🔹 The dust from the road **made it impossible to see** anything clearly.
路上的飛塵讓他們根本無法看清一切。

---

make it impossible to . . . : 致使……變得不可能
it 是受詞,用來代表 to 後面所接的內容。

ᵉ·ᵍ The noise **made it impossible to** hear him.
這些噪音讓聽他說話變得根本不可能。

22

It really was an exciting[1] time. There were so many banners[2], balloons[3], and people cheering for[4] the great politician.

On some of the banners, Ernest could see pictures of Old Stony Phiz. He thought, "He really does look like the Great Stone Face."

There was also a band[5]. It played very patriotic[6] songs and made a very festive[7] spirit[8] that day.

1. **exciting** [ɪk`saɪtɪŋ] (a.) 令人興奮的
2. **banner** [`bænər] (n.) 旗幟
3. **balloon** [bə`luːn] (n.) 氣球
4. **cheer for** 為⋯⋯歡呼
5. **band** [bænd] (n.) 樂團；樂隊
6. **patriotic** [peɪtrɪɑːtɪk] (a.) 表現愛國心的

It was very easy to join in[9] with the enthusiasm[10]. Ernest also felt very joyful[11] that

day. Even though everyone was celebrating[12], no one yet had the chance to really see Old Stony Phiz's face. But soon, more and more people got a look at[13] his face.

"Hurrah!" shouted many people. "It is Old Stony Phiz! It is the twin[14] brother of the Great Stone Face."

7. **festive** [ˋfestɪv] (a.)
   喜慶的；歡樂的
8. **spirit** [ˋspɪrɪt] (n.) 興致；情緒
9. **join in** 參加活動
10. **enthusiasm** [ɪnˋθuːzɪæzəm]
    (n.) 熱情；熱忱

11. **joyful** [ˋdʒɔɪfəl] (a.)
    充滿喜悅的
12. **celebrate** [ˋselɪbreɪt] (v.) 慶祝
13. **get a look at** 看一眼
14. **twin** [twɪn] (a.) 雙胞胎的

23

Ernest looked very carefully[1] at the man's face. "Yes," he thought. "He really does look like the face on the mountain." Ernest continued studying[2] the man's face. But something was missing[3].

When Ernest looked at the politician more closely[4], he saw a weary[5] face. He saw something empty[6] in Old Stony Phiz's face. The Great Stone Face looked complete[7]. But the politician's face did not.

1. **carefully** [ˋkɛrfəlɪ] (adv.) 仔細地；謹慎地
2. **study** [ˋstʌdɪ] (v.) 細察
3. **missing** [ˋmɪsɪŋ] (a.) 缺乏的
4. **closely** [ˋkloʊslɪ] (adv.) 仔細地
5. **weary** [ˋwɪrɪ] (a.) 疲憊的
6. **empty** [ˋɛmptɪ] (a.) 空洞的
7. **complete** [kəmˋpliːt] (a.) 完美的
8. **turn one's back on** 轉身背對

Ernest's neighbor was standing beside him. "Doesn't he look just like the Great Face?" asked the neighbor.

Ernest said, "No. He looks nothing like him."

"Well, then, that is too bad for the Great Stone Face. The politician is a great man," replied the neighbor.

Ernest turned his back on[8] the parade.

24

Again, many years passed by. Ernest grew older, and white hair started appearing[1] on his head.

He once[2] lived without[3] fame[4]. But after many years, this changed. Over the years, his wisdom deepened[5], and his good advice became famous all over the world[6].

Many people from many places came to speak to him. They came looking for[7] wisdom. People were always so impressed[8] by him.

They would[9] say, "When Ernest speaks, his face glows[10]. It is like he is more than[11] human."

1. **appear** [ə`pɪr] (v.) 出現
2. **once** [wʌns] (adv.) 曾經
3. **without** [wɪ`ðaut] (prep.) 無；沒有
4. **fame** [feɪm] (n.) 名聲
5. **deepen** [`diːpən] (v.) 加深
6. **all over the world** 遍及全世界
7. **look for** 尋找
8. **be impressed** 印象深刻
9. **would** [wud] (aux.) 總是；總會
10. **glow** [gloʊ] (v.) 發光；發熱
11. **more than** 超越；超過

And when the visitors left, they stopped to look at the Great Stone Face. Each person would say, "Someone I saw resembles this Great Stone Face." But no one could remember who.

One Point Lesson

◦ Ernest **grew older**, and white hair started appearing on his head.
恩尼斯漸漸變老，頭上開始出現白髮。

「**grow + 比較級形容詞**」：用來形容由一狀態演變成
另一狀態的過程。

e.g It **grew colder** as it became dark.
當天色變暗，天氣也變得越來越冷。

A Match.

1 My father works for the country.

He is a _____.　　　　　　　•　　•　**a** politician

2 My mother teaches at a college.

She is a _____.　　　　　　•　　•　**b** warrior

3 My brother and I were born at the same time.

He is my _____ brother.　　•　　•　**c** professor

4 My grandfather was a soldier.

He was a _____.　　　　　•　　•　**d** twin

B True or False.

T F　1 Old Stony Phiz was a brilliant speaker.

T F　2 The people in the valley elected Old Stony Phiz President.

T F　3 Ernest became a little arrogant as he grew older.

C Choose the correct answer.

❶ What did Ernest see when he looked at Great Stone Face?

(a) A complete face.

(b) A weary face.

(c) A wrinkled face.

❷ Why did many people come to Ernest?

(a) To live a simple life with him.

(b) To give him advice.

(c) To look for his knowledge and wisdom

D Fill in the blanks with the given words.

insignificant   patriotic   hopeful   joyful

❶ Old Blood-and-Thunder passed away as an _____ man to the valley.

❷ Ernest was always _____. He believed the legendary man would come.

❸ The band played very _____ songs. It was impressive.

❹ Many people were singing and dancing. It was a _____ day.

Chapter Five

The Poet

Somewhere[1] in another place, there was a poet[2]. He was originally[3] from[4] the valley of the Stone Face.

He never forgot the valley and the Great Stone Face. So he often used the beauty, peace, and simplicity[5] of that tranquil[6] place in his poems[7]. He became very famous. Everyone loved his poems.

Ernest also loved these poems. He sometimes even felt that he was the poet. The poet so often reflected[8] Ernest's own thoughts on the world.

Every evening, Ernest read these poems while sitting in front of the Great Stone Face.

Ernest looked up at[9] the Face and said, "This poet understands everything you have taught me. Is this not the man who resembles you?"

The face seemed to smile, but answered not a word.

1. **somewhere** [`sʌmwer] (adv.) 在某處
2. **poet** [`poʊət] (n.) 詩人
3. **originally** [ə`rɪdʒənəli] (adv.) 起初；原來
4. **be from** 來自
5. **simplicity** [sɪm`plɪsəti] (n.) 純樸；單純
6. **tranquil** [`træŋkwəl] (a.) 平靜的；安寧的
7. **poem** [`poʊəm] (n.) 詩
8. **reflect** [rɪ`flekt] (v.) 反映
9. **look up at** 往上看

    The poet lived very far away from the valley in a big city. But he also knew about Ernest. He had heard about him from another writer[1].

    In fact, some of his poems were developed from Ernest's character[2]. He really wanted to meet the man who gave him so much inspiration[3].

    One day, the poet decided to go to the valley of the Great Stone Face. He traveled[4] for many hours, and finally arrived at[5] the hotel Mr. Gathergold once lived in.

1. **writer** [`raɪtər] (n.) 作家
2. **character** [`kærəktər] (n.) 特質；性格
3. **inspiration** [ˌɪnspə`reɪʃən] (n.) 靈感
4. **travel** [trævəl] (v.) 旅行
5. **arrive at** 抵達
6. **along** [ə`lɔːŋ] (prep.) 沿著

The poet did not enter the hotel. Instead, he took his bag and started walking. He found a small house and asked the farmer, "Excuse me. Can you tell me where Ernest lives?"

"Of course," said the farmer. "He is my neighbor. His house is the next one along[6] this road."

27

The poet walked a short distance[1] and soon found it. He also saw Ernest sitting outside the house. He was reading a book.

"Can you give a traveler[2] a place to sleep for the night?" he asked Ernest.

Ernest looked up, smiled, and said, "Of course."

The poet sat down next to him, and they began to talk. The hours passed by like seconds.

In the poet's life, he had the chance to talk to some of the smartest men in the world. But no man was like Ernest. No man could express his deepest thoughts and feelings[3] like Ernest.

1. **distance** [ˋdɪstəns] (n.) 距離
2. **traveler** [ˋtrævələr] (n.) 旅行者
3. **feeling** [ˋfiːlɪŋ] (n.) 感覺；感受
4. **impress** [ɪmˋpres] (v.) 給……極深的印象
5. **complete** [kəmˋpliːt] (a.) 完全的；徹底的
6. **harmony** [ˋhɑːrmənɪ] (n.) 協調；一致

The poet was deeply impressed[4]. Ernest was also very impressed by the poet. He never met a man before who could understand him so well. It seemed like their thoughts were in complete[5] harmony[6].

28

Ernest looked up[1] at the Great Stone Face. He seemed to be listening to everything that Ernest and the poet were talking about.

He turned back to the poet and asked, "Who are you?"

The poet looked at the book and pointed to[2] his name on the cover[3]. He said, "You know my name. You are reading my poems."

For many years, Ernest hoped that this poet would become the human form of the Great Stone Face. He looked at the Face and then at the poet.

1. **look up** 抬頭望
2. **point to** 指向
3. **cover** [`kʌvər] (n.) 封面
4. **be surprised at** 對……感到驚訝
5. **all one's life** 一生
6. **be sorry to** 感到遺憾的
7. **disappoint** [dɪsə`pɔɪnt] (v.) 使……感到失望
8. **be worthy to** 值得的;足以……的

Ernest looked very sad and disappointed. The poet was surprised at[4] this. "Why do you suddenly look so sad?" he asked.

"All my life[5] I have waited to see the legendary human form of the Great Stone Face. I hoped you would be him."

"You hoped?" asked the poet. "You hoped I would be the human form of the Great Stone Face? I am really sorry to[6] disappoint[7] you. I am not worthy to[8] resemble this great symbol."

One Point Lesson

♦ I am not **worthy to** resemble this great symbol.
   我不足以和如此不凡的象徵相提並論。

「**be worthy to** + 動詞原形」
「**be worth** + 名詞／ V-ing」：值得……；有……的價值

I'm not **worthy to** be loved. 我不值得被愛。
      This book is **worth reading**. 這本書值得一讀。

29

Ernest was puzzled by[1] his words. "Why do you think you are not worthy? Your work[2] shows sincerity[3] and purity[4]."

The poet responded[5], "My writing has small amounts[6] of purity in it. But my writing is not the same as my life. My life does not reflect my thoughts. I lack[7] faith[8]. My writing expresses the faith I want to have."

Ernest listened very carefully to the poet. Both had tears of sadness in their eyes.

1. **be puzzled by** 因……而困惑
2. **work** [wɜːrk] (n.) 作品
3. **sincerity** [sɪnˈsɪrəti] (n.) 真誠；純真
4. **purity** [ˈpjurəti] (n.) 純潔
5. **respond** [rɪˈspɑːnd] (v.) 回答
6. **amount** [əˈmaunt] (n.) 數量
7. **lack** [læk] (v.) 沒有
8. **faith** [feɪθ] (n.) 信心；忠實
9. **give a speech** 發表演說

For a long time, Ernest had been giving speeches[9] to the local people next to a pretty forest.

He and the poet now walked to that place. There was a small forest with a tiny[10] opening[11]. They walked through the opening and there was a beautiful view[12].

They were looking out onto[13] a peaceful lake with the Great Stone Face behind it. It was magnificent[14].

10. **tiny** [ˋtaɪni] (a.) 極小的
11. **opening** [ˋoʊpnɪŋ] (n.) 空地
12. **view** [vjuː] (n.) 風景；景色
13. **onto** [ˋɑːntu] (prep.) 在……之上
14. **magnificent** [mægˋnɪfəsnət] (a.) 壯麗的；宏偉的

30

In front of them was a small gathering[1] of people. By now[2], the sun was casting[3] shadows over the Great Stone Face. It was an amazing sight[4].

The poet stood looking at the beautiful sight for many minutes. It was inspiration[5] for his next poem.

But the people were more interested in Ernest and his speech. It was such a powerful speech because his words reflected his life. He lived a life[6] of the greatest deeds[7]. The poet also listened very carefully to Ernest. His eyes were filled with[8] tears.

He thought, "His words are more beautiful and powerful than any of the poetry[9] I have written. He is like a prophet[10]."

The poet looked at Ernest. He admired[11] his gentle[12] and kind face. He admired the head of white hair. He also looked at the Great Stone Face behind Ernest.

1. **gathering** [ˋgæðərɪŋ] (n.) 聚會
2. **by now** 此刻
3. **cast** [kæst] (v.) 投射
4. **sight** [saɪt] (n.) 景象
5. **inspiration** [ɪnspəˋreɪʃən] (n.) 靈感；啟發
6. **live a life** 過生活
7. **deed** [diːd] (n.) 行為
8. **be filled with** 充滿
9. **poetry** [ˋpoʊətri] (n.) 詩（總稱）
10. **prophet** [ˋprɑːfɪt] (n.) 先知
11. **admire** [ədˋmaɪər] (v.) 欽佩；欣賞
12. **gentle** [ˋdʒentl] (a.) 和善的；仁慈的

31

Now, in the light of the evening, the final[1] rays[2] of the sun shone on the Great Face. It looked like[3] it had white hair, too. It was a very grand[4] sight.

At that moment[5], the poet realized[6] something. He looked at Ernest again. Then, he looked up to the Great Stone Face again. He felt a strange feeling in his whole body[7].

1. **final** [`faɪnəl] (a.)
   最後的；最終的
2. **ray** [reɪ] (n.) 光線
3. **look like** 看起來……
4. **grand** [grænd] (a.)
   宏大的；壯觀的

Suddenly, he threw up his arms[8] and cried out, "Everybody! Look at the Great Stone Face! Look at Ernest! He resembles the Great Stone Face!"

They said, "It is true! Ernest does resemble the Great Stone Face!"

Finally, after so many years of waiting, the legendary man was there in the valley.

Ernest turned to look at the Great Stone Face. By now, his speech was over. He just left that small gathering and walked home.

He did not believe he resembled the Great Face. He still hoped he would meet a man just like the Great Stone Face one day.

5. **at that moment** 在那一刻
6. **realize** [ˋrɪəlaɪz] (v.)
   了解；領悟
7. **whole body** 全身
8. **throw up one's arm**
   舉起手臂

A Fill in the blanks with the given words.

from	by	with	at	in	to

❶ The poet was different _____ those men.

❷ He pointed _____ his name on the cover.

❸ The poet was surprised _____ this.

❹ He is not worthy _____ resemble this great symbol.

❺ They were interested _____ his speech.

❻ His eyes were filled _____ tears.

B Who says each sentence? Circle E for Ernest and P for the Poet.

E P ❶ Can you give me a place to sleep for the night?

E P ❷ Your work shows sincerity and purity.

E P ❸ All my life I have waited to see the human form of the Great Stone Face.

E P ❹ My life does not reflect my thoughts.

C Choose the correct answer.

❶ Why did Ernest love the poems?

(a) Because they were famous all over the world.

(b) Because they were compared to an angel's singing.

(c) Because they had everything Ernest loved.

D Rearrange the sentences in chronological order.

❶ The poet traveled to Ernest's home.

❷ The poet listened to Ernest's speech with the people.

❸ The poet realized Ernest was the legendary man.

❹ Ernest and the poet shared their ideas and feelings.

_____ ⇨ _____ ⇨ _____ ⇨ _____

Appendixes

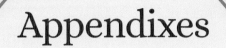

1 Basic Grammar

要增強英文閱讀理解能力，應練習找出英文的主結構。
要擁有良好的英語閱讀能力，首先要理解英文的段落結構。

「英文的主要句型結構比較簡單」

所有的英文文章都是由主詞和動詞所構成的，無論文章再怎麼長或複雜，它的架構一定是「主詞和動詞」，而「補語」和「受詞」是做補充主詞和動詞的角色。

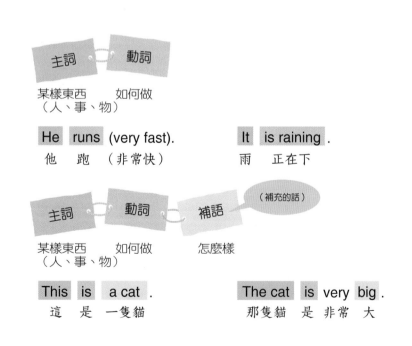

主詞　　　動詞
某樣東西　　如何做
（人、事、物）

He runs (very fast).
他　跑　（非常快）

It is raining .
雨　正在下

主詞　　　動詞　　　補語　　（補充的話）
某樣東西　　如何做　　怎麼樣
（人、事、物）

This is a cat .
這　是　一隻貓

The cat is very big .
那隻貓　是　非常　大

主詞 —— 動詞 —— 受詞

某樣東西　　　　如何做　　　　什麼
（人、事、物）

人，事物，
兩者皆是受詞

I like you .

我 喜歡 你

You gave me some flowers .

你　　給　　我　　一些花

主詞 —— 動詞 —— 受詞 —— 補語

某樣東西　　　　如何做　　　　什麼　　怎麼樣／什麼
（人、事、物）

You make me happy .　I saw him running .

你 使（讓）我 幸福（快樂）　我 看到 他　　跑

　　其他修飾語或副詞等，都可以視為為了完成句子而臨時、額外、特別附加的，閱讀起來便可更加輕鬆。先具備這些基本概念，再閱讀《人面巨石》的部分精選篇章，最後做了解文章整體架構的練習。

Deep in a valley, there was a pretty little house .

很深的山谷裡　　　　　有　　　一棟很小的房子

It was surrounded by many tall trees.

它　　被包圍　　　由許多高大的樹木

Sitting in front of their small home, a mother and her young son

　　　　坐在小房子前　　　　　一位母親和她年紀很小的兒子

were watching the sun go down .

在看　　　太陽　　下沉

"It is a very beautiful evening, isn't it?"

它 是 一個非常美麗的 傍晚 不是嗎

the mother asked the boy.

母親 問 男孩

He just nodded.

他 只 點頭

He was staring at something in the distance.

他 正凝視著 某樣東西 在遠處

Very far away, they could see the Great Stone Face.

極為遙遠 他們 可以看到 人面巨石

They were many miles from it, but they could see it clearly.

他們 是 好幾英里遠 但 他們 可以看見 它 清楚地

It was an amazing sight.

它 是 一個驚人的 景象

It looked like a sculpture of a giant in the rocks.

它 看起來 像岩石上的巨人雕像

The Face had a long nose and big lips and eyes.

那張臉 有 長鼻子和大嘴唇與眼睛

It was a very noble face.

它 是 一張非常高貴的 臉

It was easy to see this face from a distance.

它 是 容易的 從遠處看他的臉

But the further a person walked away,

但一個人走得越遠

the more clearly they could see the face .

越清楚　　他們　能看見　那張臉

People living in the area were very happy .

住在該區域的人　　是　非常　快樂

They were very proud of the Great Stone Face.

他們　是　非常　自豪　　對人面巨石

It was a famous symbol of the area.

它　是　有名的　象徵　在該區域

It was a symbol of strength, nobility, fertility and education.

它　是　一個象徵　力量、高貴、豐饒和教育

There were many stories about the Great Stone Face.

有　　很多傳說　　關於人面巨石

Some believed that the Stone Face made the land fertile .

一些人　相信　　人面巨石　讓　土地　肥沃

When the sun was needed, the sun shone .

當需要陽光時　太陽　照耀

When the rain was needed, the rain poured down .

當需要雨水時　雨　大量降下

The mother , sitting outside of her house,

母親　　坐在她的房子外

was thinking about this Stone Face.

在想　關於人面巨石

Her son , Ernest, was still staring at the Great Face .

她的兒子　恩尼斯　仍然凝視著　人面巨石

Guide to Listening Comprehension

 When listening to the story, use some of the techniques shown below. If you take time to study some phonetic characteristics of English, listening will be easier.

Get in the flow of English.

English creates a rhythm formed by combinations of strong and weak stress intonations. Each word has its particular stress that combines with other words to form the overall pattern of stress or rhythm in a particular sentence.

When you are speaking and listening to English, it is essential to get in the flow of the rhythm of English. It takes a lot of practice to get used to such a rhythm. So, you need to start by identifying the stressed syllable in a word.

Listen for the strongly stressed words and phrases.

In English, key words and phrases that are essential to the meaning of a sentence are stressed louder. Therefore, pay attention to the words stressed with a higher pitch. When listening to an English recording for the first time, what matters most is to listen for a general understanding of what you hear. Do not try to hear every single word. Most of the unstressed words are articles or auxiliary verbs, which don't play an important role in the general context. At this level, you can ignore them.

Pay attention to liaisons.

In reading English, words are written with a space between them. There isn't such an obvious guide when it comes to listening to English. In oral English, there are many cases when the sounds of words are linked with adjacent words.

For instance, let's think about the phrase "**take off**," which can be used in "take off your clothes." "Take off your clothes" doesn't sound like [teɪk ɔːf] with each of the words completely and clearly separated from the others. Instead, it sounds as if almost all the words in context are slurred together, [ˈteɪkɔːf], for a more natural sound.

Shadow the voice of the native speaker.

Finally, you need to mimic the voice of the native speaker. Once you are sure you know how to pronounce all the words in a sentence, try to repeat them like an echo. Listen to the book again, but this time you should try a fun exercise while listening to the English.

This exercise is called "shadowing." The word "shadow" means a dark shade that is formed on a surface. When used as a verb, the word refers to the action of following someone or something like a shadow. In this exercise, pretend you are a parrot and try to shadow the voice of the native speaker.

Try to mimic the reader's voice by speaking at the same speed, with the same strong and weak stresses on words, and pausing or stopping at the same points.

Experts have already proven this technique to be effective. If you practice this shadowing exercise, your English speaking and listening skills will improve by leaps and bounds. While shadowing the native speaker, don't forget to pay attention to the meaning of each phrase and sentence.

Step 1 Listen to what you want to shadow many times. Start out by just trying to shadow a few words or a sentence.

 Step 2 Mimic the CD out loud. You can shadow everything the speaker says as if you are singing a round, or you also can speak simultaneously with the recorded voice of the native speaker.

 Step 3 As you practice more, try to shadow more. For instance, shadow a whole sentence or paragraph instead of just a few words.

3 Listening Guide

以下為《人面巨石》各章節的前半部。一開始若能聽清楚發音，之後就沒有聽力的負擔。先聽過摘錄的章節，之後再反覆聆聽括弧內單字的發音，並仔細閱讀各種發音的說明。

以下都是以英語的典型發音為基礎，所做的簡易說明，即使這裡未提到的發音，也可以配合音檔反覆聆聽，如此一來聽力必能更上層樓。

Chapter One page 14 🎧 32

(**❶**) (　　　　) a valley, there was a (**❷**) little house. It was surrounded by many tall trees. Sitting (**❸**) (　　　) (　　　　) their small home, a mother and her young son were watching the sun go down.

❶ Deep in: deep 的 p 和 in 會像同一個單字般連在一起發音，發出像 deeping 的連音，屬於常出現的發音型態，讀者應熟記此類發音法。

❷ pretty: 唸 pretty 的時候，原來無聲的 -tty 會接近有聲的 -ddy 音。

❸ in front of: in front of 是常使用的介系詞片語，應熟記 front 和 of 是發連音，-nt 的 [t] 發音不會太重，與 -nt 相連的單字，[t] 音省略不發出來是美語的特徵。

One day, (❶) was working in his fields. Suddenly, a neighbor came to him and asked, " (❷) ( ) hear the news?"

"No. What news?" Ernest replied. The neighbor continued, "People say that there is a (❸) man in Newport. He looks like the Great Stone Face."

❶ **Ernest:** 重音在第一音節，Er 發捲舌音，整個字的正確發音為 [ɜːrnɪst]，但字尾的 -st 因為發音較為不順，口語中常會將 [t] 音迅速帶過。

❷ **Did you:** 以 -d 為字尾的單字與 you 連接時，會形成連音 ju 或 ja，在非正式場合或說得很快的時候，did 的音甚至會聽不見。

❸ **great:** great 字尾的 -t 因為受到前面連著母音的影響，唸的時候會由無聲的 [t] 音變得比較像有聲的 [d] 音。本句中 great man 兩個單字連在一起發音時，[t] 音則會迅速略過，聽不太出來。

Many years ago, (❶) man grew up in the valley. This man left home, and (❷) (   ) army. He became a great soldier. After many years of life in the army, he became a (❸). He was called Old Blood-and-Thunder. He was now very old.

❶ **another:** 重音在第二音節，字首 a- 的發音很微弱，有時在句中有前後文時甚至不發音，而整個單字只發出 -nother 的音。

❷ **joined the:** joined 的發音原本為 [dʒɔɪnd]，但與 the 放在一起時，[d] 往往會省略聽不清楚，因此要仔細聆聽前後文來分辨時態。

❸ **general:** 重音在第一音節，第一音節中的 -e 發 [e] 的音，字尾的 -al 發音則是以舌尖頂至上顎的 [ə] 音。

Chapter Four page 58 🎧35

Like Mr. Gathergold, Old (❶)-(   )-(   ) passed away as (❷) insignificant man for the valley.
Now, many people said, "Old Blood-and-Thunder did not really resemble the Great Stone Face. We were foolish to think so."

❶ Blood-and-Thunder: 這三個連字的重音在第三個字 thunder。blood 和 and 變成連音，and 輕輕發音即可，連接詞、介系詞或冠詞在句子裡通常不太重要，因此發音很微弱，快速略過即可。

❷ an: an 在不同的位置會有不同的發音，作為不定冠詞的正常發音為 [ən]，若要強調時發較重的 [æ] 音。

Chapter Five page 72 🎧 36

(**❶**) in another place, there was a poet. He was (**❷**) from the valley of the Great Stone Face. He never forgot the valley and the Great Stone Face. So he often (**❸**) ( ) beauty, peace, and simplicity of that tranquil place in his poems.

❶ Somewhere: 重音在第一音節，其中 -wh- 發 [w] 音。

❷ originally: 重音在第二音節，字首的 o 發音很輕，有時在對話中會聽不出來，但名詞的 origin 重音就在第一音節，-o 發 [ə] 的音。

❸ used the: used 的字尾 -ed 發 [d] 的音，但與其他單字連在一起時發音很弱，甚至不發音，這種情況類似 joined the 的發音方式，必須聽清楚上下文才能判斷其時態。

4

Listening Comprehension

🎧 37 **A** Listen to the CD and fill in the blanks.

1 He looks like the Great Stone Face.
People _____ him Mr. Gathergold.

2 My life does not reflect my _____.

3 The furniture, carpets and curtains are all _____.

4 It is the _____ brother of the Great Stone Face.

5 I hope Mr. Gathergold is the _____ man.

6 Look at Ernest! He _____ the Great Stone Face!

7 Did you hear the _____ about the Great Stone Face?

🎧 38 **B** True or False.

T F **1** _____

T F **2** _____

T F **3** _____

T F **4** _____

T F **5** _____

39 **C** Listen to the CD and choose the correct answer.

1 _____?

    (a) He wasn't kind or generous.

    (b) He was too old.

    (c) He had too much money.

    (d) His house was too big.

2 _____?

    (a) He didn't write any books.

    (b) He only wore a green uniform.

    (c) He was not wise.

    (d) He was not a man of peace.

40 **D** Match.

1 _____ •

2 _____ •

3 _____ •

4 _____ •

• **a** who looked like the Great Stone Face.

• **b** but he was so smart.

• **c** he became a general.

• **d** he was always hopeful.

Translation

霍桑

（Nathaniel Hawthorne, 1804–1864）

　　霍桑是美國作家，生長在極度嚴格的清教家庭。童年時期，霍桑便對閱讀萌生興趣。大學畢業後，他開始寫作生涯，為家鄉的期刊貢獻了許多文章與短篇小說。

　　1837 年，第一本小說問世，建立了霍桑在文壇的重要地位。他持續著作，於 1850 年發表《紅字》（*The Scarlet Letter*）。

　　霍桑致力探查人性罪惡與良知之間的互動，並以此聞名，為反人性的邪惡與內在衝突提供洞見。

　　延續祖先們的清教傳統，霍桑謹慎地處理人性充滿罪愆的本質。他以道德、宗教與心理學的角度，檢視個體在自私孤獨與腐敗下的心理狀態與行為。

　　《人面巨石》內容追求人類的理想形象，是霍桑晚年著作的短篇小說。一個叫恩尼斯的男孩從母親那裡聽說，有個將誕生的嬰孩，會注定成為時代的偉人，並且相貌會與山壁碩石形成的人面巨石像完全相同。

　　恩尼斯誠摯儉樸地生活，等待巨石的面貌化成人類出現。時光流逝，他遇見富有的商人、偉大的軍人和詩人，但沒有一人長得和巨石有絲毫相像。

　　有天，一位詩人望著向村人演說的恩尼斯，高喊：「看看恩尼斯，他和人面巨石一模一樣！」然而，回家途中，恩尼斯仍祈禱能有比自己更睿智、更好、貌同人面巨石的人出現。

　　霍桑的許多作品具有道德主題，《人面巨石》即為其一。一個好人的價值並非來自舉世名聲、金銀財富或權力威勢，而是在於對自我的持續觀照中體現，因為一個人的言論想法，應與日常生活的行動一致。

[第一章] 山谷中的男孩

p. 14–15 在深山谷中，有一棟很小的屋子，周圍環繞著許多高大的樹木。就在小屋前，有位母親與年幼的兒子正在觀賞著日落。

「這真是個美麗的黃昏，不是嗎？」母親問小男孩。他點點頭。他正盯著遠方的某樣東西。

他們可以在很遠很遠的地方，就看到那一塊人面巨石。就算距離個幾英里遠，還是可以看得很清楚。

那是一個奇景，看起來就彷彿岩石上刻著一個巨人的雕像。雕像的臉上有長長的鼻子、大大的嘴唇和一雙眼睛，相貌極為尊貴。

p. 16–17 只要隔著一定的距離，就能看到這張臉，只不過離得愈遠能看得愈清楚。

住在這附近的人都覺得很幸福，他們以人面巨石為傲，它是當地的著名景觀，代表著力量、高貴、豐饒和學識。

許許多多的故事都與人面巨石有關。有些人相信，是人面巨石使這片土地變得豐饒：當他們需要太陽，陽光便為他們閃耀；當他們需要雨水，大雨便傾瀉而下。

這母親就站在屋外，想著人面巨石的故事，而兒子恩尼斯仍一直盯著人面巨石看。

p. 18-19 男孩轉過身說：「媽媽，人面巨石看起來既慈祥又有智慧，如果他會說話，他的聲音一定會很溫柔，我真希望能夠認識像他這樣的人。」

「有一個古老的故事曾經傳說，將來有一天，會誕生出一個像他那樣的人。你聽過這個故事嗎？」

男孩興奮地說：「沒有，媽媽！我沒有聽過，拜託妳告訴我吧。」

母親開始對兒子訴說這個故事。

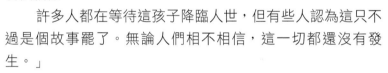

「這發生在非常遙遠的過去，很久以前，這片山谷中住了很多的印地安人，他們深信，有一天，會誕生出一個有著不凡命運的孩子，這孩子會是最聰明、最富有，也最高貴的一個人，會長得和人面巨石很相像。

許多人都在等待這孩子降臨人世，但有些人認為這只不過是個故事罷了。無論人們相不相信，這一切都還沒有發生。」

p. 20-21 男孩仔細地聽母親說著。「媽媽，我很希望這會發生，我想認識這個人，我知道我一定會很喜歡他的。」

男孩的母親並不相信這個故事，但是她想給兒子一些希望，便說道：「也許可以喔，也許這很快就會發生了。」

小男孩從未忘記這件事，每一天，他醒來後就凝望著人面巨石，希望自己能遇到長得像人面巨石那樣的人。

恩尼斯是個很乖的小男孩，他很愛母親，都會幫忙做家事，也很聽母親的話，但其實他給母親的最大幫助，就是他對母親的愛。

p. 22–23 很快地，恩尼斯長大了，他大半時間都在田裡工作。他很重感情，為人忠誠，也很聰明。

他沒有受過良好的教育，但有些人會説：「恩尼斯真是聰明，很多男孩去唸名校，但是都不如恩尼斯聰明。他智慧淵博，有一天，會成為一個偉大的人的。」

在結束一整天辛勞的工作後，恩尼斯往往會跑去看人面巨石像，他會靜靜坐在那兒好幾個小時，就只是看著它。

在這段時間裡，他思考許多事情，對生命也漸漸有更清楚的認識。

他坐在那兒思索著怨恨、痛苦、嫉妒等等生命中的各種問題，其中最重要的課題便是愛，而他也培養出一種平靜仁慈態度來對待萬物。

[第二章] 富有的商人

p. 26–27 有一天，恩尼斯在自家田裡工作，一個鄰居突然跑來問他：「你聽到消息了嗎？」

「沒耶，什麼消息？」恩尼斯回答。

鄰居繼續説：「人們説啊，紐波特住了一個偉大的人物，他長得跟人面巨石很像，大家稱他為聚金先生，不過我想這應該不是他的真名。反正呢，他很久以前是住在這個山谷裡的，後來才搬去紐波特開創事業的。」

聽到這個消息，恩尼斯很興奮，他問道：「為什麼人們要叫他做『聚金先生』？」

鄰居說：「這個嘛，在很久以前，他還一貧如洗，他的創業資金才一點點，但他很聰明，賺了很多錢，和世界各地的人做生意。他從非洲帶回黃金和鑽石，從亞洲買了地毯，還帶了香料、各種茶葉和珍珠回來。」

p. 28–29 「他的事業非常成功，」鄰居繼續說道，「有些人甚至把他比喻成邁達斯，你知道希臘神話裡的邁達斯吧？他能夠點石成金。有人就說啊，只要是聚金先生碰到的東西，也都會變成黃金，反正現在山谷裡流傳著這個消息，說不定聚金先生會回到這裡。」
　　恩尼斯聽得興致勃勃。
　　「他現在很有錢了，我聽說他可能會回到這片他生長的山谷，蓋一棟大房子。你知道強生家旁邊那片美麗河畔吧？很久以前，聚金先生就是在那兒長大的，人們說他打算在那裡蓋一棟大房子。」
　　「真的嗎？」恩尼斯說，「我想見見這個人，希望他真的和人面巨石長得很像。」

p. 30–31 好幾個星期過去了，許多建築工人來到山谷，開始建造河邊大宅。好多人前來看他們興建這幢驚人的豪宅。
　　好幾個月過去，房子落成了，成為了山谷裡最熱門的話題。
　　「你看過那棟房子了嗎？」人們問恩尼斯。

　　「有，我看過了。」恩尼斯回答。「真是太了不起了吧？聚金先生一定就是我們在等待的那個人。」

這棟建築物的確驚人。從遠處看，它像是銀光閃耀的星星。如果走近一點，就會看見門前高大的石柱，石柱的材質是價格昂貴的大理石。

屋前巨大的門，是由高級的進口木材所製，門把也極其華麗。

p. 32-33 每個人都對這棟豪宅感到非常好奇。「不知道屋子裡頭是長什麼樣子的？」他們很想知道。

一位建築工人說道：「裡面還比外面更漂亮呢，裡面的家具、地毯、窗簾，全都是國外進口的。聚金先生的臥室尤其富麗，到處都是黃金做的東西，金光閃耀，我猜要是沒有金子在身邊，他就睡不著吧。」

包括恩尼斯在內，大家都準備著迎接聚金先生，認為他就是傳說故事裡的那個人，他們都在等待他的到來。

山谷裡，許多人都在問：「他什麼時候會來？」

「他預計今天傍晚會抵達。」其他人回答。

所有人都等不及了，恩尼斯也是，他渴望見到一張與人面巨石一樣的面孔，那個他喜愛的人面巨石。

恩尼斯想，「等他來到這裡，他會為山谷做出許多貢獻，他很富有，可以做一些了不起的事。」

p. 34-35 夕陽西下，人們聚集在一起等待這位名人到來，恩尼斯也在其中。這時，傳來了車輪沿路轉動的聲音。

「他來了！他來了！」人們喊叫著，「他終於來了！」

當馬車經過，恩尼斯看到了聚金先生。聚金先生年紀很大了，眼睛很小，有著薄薄的嘴唇。

「他看起來就和人面巨石一模一樣。」有些人大喊著，「從現在起，好事會降臨我們山谷！」

恩尼斯看著馬車沿路往前行駛。在馬車前方，有一位老婦人和兩名小孩在路邊行乞。

當馬車經過他們身邊時，恩尼斯看到一隻蠟黃的手伸出窗外，丟了幾個銅板到他們面前。

此刻恩尼斯覺得十分失望。

p. 36–37 但是人們依然喊叫著：「他看起來就和人面巨石一模一樣！」

恩尼斯想：「他的外表看起來或許很像人面巨石，但是他的心卻毫無相似之處。這位老人看起來冷酷又自私，但是人面巨石是寬大又富同情心的。」

接著他轉身望著人面巨石，在那一刻它似乎在對他說話，它說：「別擔心，恩尼斯，總有一天，傳說中的人物會到來的。」

許多年過去了，恩尼斯已經是成年人了，但是他每天依然會望著人面巨石一會兒。

事實上，有些人這麼說：「恩尼斯還是花那麼多時間看人面巨石，真是太蠢了！」

也有其他人說：「隨他吧，反正他也沒有因此荒廢工作。」

p. 38–39 但沒有人真正了解恩尼斯。人面巨石教了他許多事，那些他所明白的事理，是不可能從書上學到的。

因為人面巨石的啟發，他慢慢累積知識，發展出獨特的生活方式與人格。

他是世上最有智慧的人之一，但他自己都還沒發現到。

許多年過去，有一天，聚金先生過世了，在去世之前，他所有的金錢財產全都消耗殆盡。

大家都在想：「他的錢都花去哪裡了？」但是這些疑問從未得到解答。過了一段日子，人們再也不拿他和人面巨石相比了。

最後，他的名聲完全只來自一個理由——他的豪宅。現在房子變成了一間旅館，到了夏天，許多人留宿那裡，要去看人面巨石。

［第三章］偉大的軍人

p. 44–45 很多年前，也有另一位男子在山谷裡成長，後來他離開家鄉參軍，成為一名偉大的軍人。

在經歷多年的軍旅生涯後，他成為將軍，人人都稱他為鐵血將軍。現在，他垂垂老矣，身上到處都是戰爭中留下的傷疤，先前他已從軍職退休，並決定回到他山谷中的家園。

有一天，恩尼斯與鄰居正在閒聊。

「你有聽到最近的傳聞嗎，恩尼斯？」鄰居問道。

「有，他們說老將軍簡直長得和人面巨石一模一樣，」恩尼斯說，「是真的嗎？」

「嗯，我也不知道，但是將軍的手下來過這裡，他說將軍看起來就像人面巨石。」鄰居回答。

「那我們就只好等他來到這裡了。」恩尼斯說。

p. 46–47 當地市民決定為鐵血將軍辦一場盛大歡迎會。這天到來時，所有居民都進城參加慶祝，恩尼斯也來觀看這場盛會。

這是一場很棒的歡迎會，桌上準備了豐盛的筵席，令人垂涎三尺。從這裡，人們也能看到遠方的人面巨石。

恩尼斯看到會場聚集了許多人，還聽到貝特布雷斯教士發表演說。他踮起腳尖，想要看鐵血將軍，但人實在太多只好作罷，他轉頭望向人面巨石，看著石臉上的微笑，讓他心裡又覺得舒暢起來。

p. 48–49 恩尼斯在人群後方站了好一會兒。就在他看著人面巨石之際，他聽見周圍許多人的對話。

其中一人說道：「他看起來就跟人面巨石一樣！」

他還聽見其他人說：「鐵血將軍就是最了不起的偉人，他就是人面巨石。」

這些人開始歡呼喝采：「好啊！」其他人也同樣激動地歡呼起來。

聽了大家的對話後，恩尼斯心想：「這人一定就是人面巨石的化身，一定沒錯！」

然而，恩尼斯先前沒料到人面巨石會是個好戰之士，他原本期待的是愛好和平的人，一位充滿智慧和見識的人。但他又想：「即使愛好戰爭之人，仍能做出不凡之事。」

p. 50-51 過沒多久,恩尼斯聽到有人大喊:「將軍!是將軍來了!他馬上要發表演說,各位,請安靜一點。」群眾立刻安靜下來。

終於,將軍站出來,每個人都見到他了。鐵血將軍開始發表演說,但是恩尼斯並沒有認真聽他說話。他看看將軍的臉,再看看他身上所穿的軍服,閃著刺眼的光芒。軍服是深綠色的,上頭還掛著許許多多的徽章。恩尼斯觀察了一會兒後想:「他真的像人面巨石嗎?」

p. 52-53 在將軍身後,恩尼斯看見的是人面巨石像。他看著那張他所喜愛的臉孔,想道:「它的臉孔充滿智慧、仁慈寬厚,鐵血將軍的臉上找不到一絲這些特質,他並不是傳說之人,我們還得再等下去。」

恩尼斯離開會場,返回家中。

那天傍晚,他又坐下看著人面巨石。

陽光在雲層中閃耀,在人面巨石上撒下陰影,在它臉上製造出微笑的表情。

這讓恩尼斯心裡舒坦了些,他彷彿聽到人面巨石在他心裡頭說著:「別擔心,恩尼斯,他會來的。」

p. 54-55 又過了多年,恩尼斯的年紀漸長,現已邁入中年,但他仍是那心地純良的恩尼斯,每個認識他的人都喜愛他,然而現在的他更富智慧了。

他一直盡力幫助他人,他的善良不只表現在行為上,也流露於言談中。他總是和善地與人交談,也為遭遇困難的人提供中肯的建議。

他言語中表現的真實無人能及。

人人都愛恩尼斯,但卻沒人真正認識到他是一位不凡人物。

[第四章] 著名的政治家

p. 58-59 和聚金先生一樣，年老的鐵血將軍在山谷中與世長辭，辭世時無人聞問。如今，人們都說：「老鐵血將軍其實一點也不像人面巨石，我們太笨了，才會信以為真。」

沒過多久，又有新消息傳出，人們談論著又有一位很像人面巨石的人。

這人過去同樣在山谷長大，現在是一名政治家。這個新出現的人物，人們稱他為「老石面」。這人不富裕，也不是軍人，而是個出色的演說家。

他說話清晰有條理，參加任何辯論無不致勝。在政府機關裡，他一開口，人們便會駐足聆聽。老石面備受舉國敬重。

p. 60-61 現在，老石面想要成為總統。甚至在這之前，就已經有人在傳：「你見過老石面嗎？他看起來和人面巨石幾乎一模一樣。」

如今人們滿懷希望老石面就是傳說人物。

一天，恩尼斯正在田裡工作，鄰居跑了過來。

「恩尼斯！」鄰居說道，「你有沒有聽到最新消息？」

恩尼斯答：「有啊，他們說老石面看起來很像人面巨石。」

「他很可能就是傳說中的人，你知道吧。」鄰居說。

恩尼斯想了想說：「嗯，不過之前的聚金先生和鐵血將軍都不是傳說人物，我們還是得等一等，觀察一下。」

說完，恩尼斯又回去繼續田裡的工作了。

p. 62–63 在老石面競選總統期間，他到了刻著人面巨石的山谷。他來到這裡的原因，只是為了拉選票，但是山谷居民為他準備了一場盛大的慶祝會。

　　同時居民還安排一場精采的遊行，那天，所有人都放下手邊工作，跑去看老石面，恩尼斯也去了，即使先前失望連連，但他仍舊懷抱著希望。

　　到鎮上的路旁沿路聚集了許多群眾。

　　人們等了一陣子，那位偉大的人物出現了，他和其他的大人物一同沿路騎著馬。但那兒聚集了太多人潮，再加上在泥地上騎馬的人也很多，飛揚的灰塵讓人們什麼都看不清楚。

p. 64–65 這真是令人興奮的時刻，到處都是旗幟和氣球，人們為這位偉大的政治家慶祝歡呼。

　　在一些旗幟上，恩尼斯看到了老石面的畫像，他想，「他看起來真的很像人面巨石。」

　　會場還有樂團在演奏愛國歌曲，讓那天充滿節慶的歡樂氛圍。

　　大家很快就融入這股熱鬧的氣氛，恩尼斯那天也很開心。大家忙著慶祝，沒有機會仔細瞧見老石面的臉孔，但沒過多久，就有越來越多人看到他了。

　　「好啊！」許多人喊叫著，「就是老石面！他和人面巨石簡直就是雙胞胎。」

p. 66–67 恩尼斯仔細看著他的臉，「沒錯，」他心想，「他的確和山上的人面巨石很像。」他繼續觀察那張臉，卻發現漏看了一點。

當他更仔細端詳著老石面，他看到的是一張疲憊的臉，老石面的臉上略顯得空洞。人面巨石看起來完美，政治家的臉卻迥然不同。

站在一旁的鄰居問道：「他看起來還是不是很像人面巨石吧？」

恩尼斯說，「不像，看起來一點也不像。」

「好吧，那麼，這對人面巨石來說真是可惜了，這位政治家可是一位很偉大的人物呢。」鄰居回應。

恩尼斯轉身離開遊行隊伍。

p. 68–69 又是許多年過去了，恩尼斯也漸漸衰老，頭上開始長出白髮。

過去他沒沒無聞，但多年後，事態開始有了轉變。歷經多年，他的智慧漸長，而他所提出的那些睿智忠告也舉世聞名。

許多人從各地前來與他交談，尋找智慧，也都對他留下了深刻的印象。

他們會說：「恩尼斯一開口，就顯得容光煥發，彷彿他已超越了人類的智慧。」

訪客在離開之際，會停下腳步望著人面巨石，而每個人都會說：「我見過有人長得和人面巨石很像。」只不過，沒人記起那人到底是誰。

[第五章] 詩人

p. 72-73 有個地方的詩人也是來自人面巨石的那片山谷。

他從未忘記家鄉的山谷與人面巨石像，因此他常在詩中描繪那片土地的美好、寧靜與純樸。他十分出名，人人都愛他寫的詩。

恩尼斯也愛這些詩作，有時他甚至覺得自己就是那名詩人，因為他的詩中總是道出恩尼斯對世事的看法。

每天傍晚，恩尼斯會坐在人面巨石像前閱讀這些詩。他抬起頭，看著石像説道：「這個詩人懂得你所教我的一切，這不就是那個像你的人嗎？」

巨石彷彿露出微笑，以無言回答了他。

p. 74-75 詩人住在距離山谷極為遙遠的大城市裡，但他也知道恩尼斯這個人，他從另一位作家那裡所聽聞。

其實，他所寫的一些詩，就是從恩尼斯身上得到啟發的。他很想見見這個為他帶來許多靈感的人物。

終於有一天，詩人決定前往那片有著人面巨石的山谷。經過許多小時的旅程，他終於抵達曾是聚金先生住家的那間旅館。

詩人並未踏入旅館，反而拾起背包開始往前走。他來到一棟小屋旁，向農夫問道：「不好意思，可以請您告訴我恩尼斯住在哪裡嗎？」

「當然。」農夫回答。「他是我的鄰居，沿著這條路走，下一棟屋子就是了。」

p. 76–77 詩人走了一小段路，很快就找到了恩尼斯的家，還看見恩尼斯就坐在屋外正在看書。

「請問可以借住一宿，讓旅人晚上有棲身之所嗎？」他問恩尼斯。

恩尼斯抬起頭，微笑道：「當然可以。」

詩人在他身旁坐下，兩人聊了起來，這段時間過得飛快。

詩人過去曾有機會與一些絕頂聰明的人物交談過，但沒有人如同恩尼斯一樣。無人能像恩尼斯這般能傳達如此深刻的思想與情感。

詩人十分佩服恩尼斯。恩尼斯也對詩人留下深刻的印象。過去他從未遇過能這麼了解他的人，他們的想法似乎極為契合。

p. 78–79 恩尼斯望著人面巨石，人面巨石彷彿正在聆聽著他與詩人的所有對話。

他轉過頭對著詩人問道：「你是誰？」

詩人看著那本書，指著印在封面上的名字。

他說：「你知道我的名字，你正在讀我寫的詩。」

多年來，恩尼斯一直希望這名詩人就是人面巨石的化身，他看看巨石，再看看詩人。

恩尼斯貌似極傷心與失望。詩人驚訝地問，「為什麼你突然間看起來這麼傷心？」

「我這一生都在期待看見傳說中面巨石的化身，我本來希望你就是那個人。」

「你希望？」詩人問，「你希望我就是和人面巨石一樣的人？很抱歉讓你失望了，我是不足以和偉大的人面巨石相提並論的。」

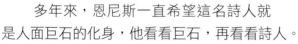

p. 80–81 恩尼斯對他的話感到疑惑,「為什麼你會覺得自己不配?你的作品充滿了誠懇與純淨的思想。」

詩人回應道:「我的作品是包含一些純淨的思想,但我的作品不代表我的生活,我的生活並沒有反映在作品中,我不夠忠實,我的作品表達的是我希望擁有的誠實特質。」

恩尼斯仔細聽著詩人的描述,兩人眼中都泛著悲傷的淚光。

長久以來,恩尼斯都在這片美麗森林邊,對當地居民發表演說。

現在,他與詩人一同踏上那片土地,那裡有片小森林,林間有一塊小空地。兩人穿過空地,眼前是一幕絕美的景色。

他們望向人面巨石前方一片寧靜的湖泊,景色十分壯麗宏偉。

p. 82–83 在他們的前方,聚集著一小群人。此刻,陽光將陰影灑在人面巨石的臉上,呈現出奇異的景象。

詩人佇足良久,凝望著美景,這會是他下一首詩的靈感來源。

不過人們對恩尼斯和他的演說更感興趣。他的演說很有說服力,因為那反映了他的生活經驗,他過著一種高尚的生活。詩人也細細聆聽恩尼斯的演說,雙眼盈滿了淚水。

他想:「他的話語比我的詩更美好,更有力量,他就好比是個先知。」

詩人望著恩尼斯,讚嘆他慈祥柔和的臉龐和他滿頭的華髮,然後又看了看恩尼斯身後的人面巨石。

p. 84–85 此刻，夕陽的餘暉照耀著人面巨石，看起來彷彿也是一頭白髮，面容莊嚴。

那一刻，詩人豁然開朗，他看看恩尼斯，再抬頭望向人面巨石，內心油然生起一股奇異的感覺。

突然間，他舉起雙臂高喊著：「各位！看看人面巨石！看看恩尼斯！他就和人面巨石一模一樣！」

人們回應：「真的耶！恩尼斯就長得和人面巨石一樣！」

終於，經過漫長的等待，傳說中的那個人就在山谷中。

恩尼斯轉身看著人面巨石。現在，他的演說結束，他離開群眾的聚會，走回家中。

他不相信自己長得像人面巨石，他依然希望，終有一天，自己能遇到和人面巨石長得一模一樣的那個人。

Answers

P. 24

A fertility, nobility, education

B ❶ F ❷ T ❸ F ❹ T

P. 25

C ❶ (b) ❷ (b)

D ❶ staring at ❷ waited for

P. 40

A ❶ A business. ❷ From Africa. ❸ Midas.

B ❶ wealthy ❷ huge ❸ expensive.

P. 41

C ❶ T ❷ T ❸ F

D ❶ palace ❷ star ❸ wood ❹ knobs

P. 56

A ❶ angel ❷ forest ❸ form.

B ❶ (b) ❷ (b)

P. 57

C ❶ E ❷ O ❸ E ❹ O

D ❶ he would be a man of war
❷ with many trees behind the chairs and table

P. 70

A ❶ -(a) ❷ -(c) ❸ -(d) ❹ -(b)

B ❶ T ❷ T ❸ F

P. 71

C ❶ (a) ❷ (c)

D ❶ insignificant ❷ hopeful ❸ patriotic
❹ joyful

P. 86

A
① from
② to/at
③ at/by
④ to
⑤ in
⑥ with

B
① P
② E
③ E
④ P

P. 87

C
① (c)

D
① → ④ → ② → ③

P. 102

A
① call
② thoughts
③ imported
④ twin
⑤ legendary
⑥ resembles
⑦ story

B
① It was easy to see this face from a distance. (T)
② There was an old story that a man like him would be born one day. (T)
③ Ernest studied hard so he could not help his mother when he was young. (F)
④ Ernest really enjoyed the festival to welcome Old Blood-and-Thunder home. (F)
⑤ When Ernest got older, he became wiser. (T)

P. 103

C
① Why wasn't Mr. Gathergold the human form of the Great Stone Face? (a)
② Why wasn't Old Blood-and-Thunder the human form of the Great Stone Face? (d)

D
① Ernest did not have a good education, - ⓑ
② Even though there were many disappointments, - ⓓ
③ After many years of life in the army, - ⓒ
④ He hoped he would meet the man - ⓐ

125

Adaptors of The Great Stone Face

Louise Benette
Macquarie University (MA, TESOL)
Sookmyung Women's University, English
Instructor

David Hwang
Michigan State University (MA, TESOL)
Ewha Womans University, English Chief Instructor,
CEO at EDITUS

人面巨石【二版】
The Great Stone Face

作者 _ 霍桑
　　　（Nathaniel Hawthorne）

改寫 _ Louise Benette, David Hwang

插圖 _ Petra Hanzak

翻譯／編輯 _ 羅竹君

作者／故事簡介翻譯 _ 王采翎

校對 _ 王采翎

協力校對 _ 洪巧玲

封面設計 _ 林書玉

排版 _ 葳豐／林書玉

播音員 _ Michael Yancey, Fiona Steward

製程管理 _ 洪巧玲

發行人 _ 周均亮

出版者 _ 寂天文化事業股份有限公司

電話 _ +886-2-2365-9739

傳真 _ +886-2-2365-9835

網址 _ www.icosmos.com.tw

讀者服務 _ onlineservice@icosmos.com.tw

出版日期 _ 2020年4月 二版一刷（250201）

郵撥帳號 _ 1998620-0 寂天文化事業股份有限公司

國家圖書館出版品預行編目資料

人面巨石 / Nathaniel Hawthorne 原著；Louise
Benette, David Hwang 改寫 . -- 二版 . -- [臺北市]
: 寂天文化 , 2020.04
　　面；　　公分 . -- (Grade 2 經典文學讀本)
譯自：The great atone face
ISBN 978-986-318-907-7(25K 平裝附光碟片)
1. 英語 2. 讀本

805.18　　　　　　　　　　　　　　109004149